Note from the author

This book is one of a series of Mr. Willow's interactive educational books with a "Foodie Flavour". They are written for an adult and child to share.

Mr. Willow's Children's Books will support you in the education of your child and make it fun! Each book provides an appropriate poem, a wealth of educational material and related activities, suggestions to extend your child's interests and a video link to support.

Current research* now emphasises the importance of the very special and intimate interactions that occur between a parent/carer and their child when reading or engaged in sustained and shared activities together. This kind of investment in your child has not only been found to benefit their social and emotional chances in life, but to positively influence their educational development, enabling them to flourish. We also know that healthy eating in the early years sets the eating patterns in future years; so influencing not only their immediate health and development, but their long term well-being and longevity.

I hope that you find this book to be informative and inspiring. I hope that it encourages discussion and offers you many opportunities to extend your child's learning and vocabulary.

I would like to thank my family and my staff at Willow Cottage Nursery for their active support in making this book possible.

Valerie

This book is dedicated to my mother Beryl whose cookery and tasty food inspired my passion for delivering and teaching children about healthy food.

*The Millennium Cohort Study 2010

Here is Mr. Willow (The Bear Chef)

When Mr Willow was a little bear he used to spend many hours gardening with his Grandad.

Can you see the picture of Grandad Willow?

Mr. Willow learnt how to grow his own fruit and vegetables and how tasty they are to eat.

Grandad Willow explained that vegetables and fruit contain lots of vitamins and minerals that help us to grow, be strong and to keep well.

Now-a-days Mr. Willow has his own little garden. Can you see it? He loves growing his own fruit and vegetables, which are very tasty to eat.

Carrots are one of Mr. Willow's favourite **ROOT** vegetables. Do you know the names of any other root vegetables?

Yes, there are parsnips, turnips, swedes, yam, beetroot, raddish, celeriac and many more. Can you spot some when you go to the shops? Can you guess why they are called root vegetables?

Yes, because they grow underground from the root of the plant. Mr. Willow knows that carrots help him to keep well and are very good for his eyes. They can even help him to see in the dark!

Mr. Willow likes eating crunchy carrots at anytime of the day. Sometimes he eats them for a snack, sometimes for his lunch and sometimes for his dinner.

He even makes carrot drinks, carrot soup, carrot cakes, and carrot puddings! Mr. Willow knows that carrots are very good for him.

So as you can imagine, Mr. Willow needs to grow lots of carrots! He prepares his little garden and sows the carrots seeds.

Then he looks after them while they grow, and waters them very carefully; not too much and not too little.

He watches how the seeds grow. The leaves grow up and the roots grow down.

Cassava

Turnips

Celeriac

Raddish

Parsnip

Beetroot

Here is
Mr. Willow's
special poem
about carrots;
it is called

Carrots are very good for you...
...don't you know!

Down in his garden,
neatly in a row

That's where Mr Willow's
crunchy carrots grow!

" Carrots are very good for you...
...don't you know!"

He sows
the seeds
and waters
them well,

out comes the
sun and the seeds
begin to swell.

Up pop the shoots; the leaves begin to grow!

"Carrots are very good for you...
Mr.Willow
...don't you know!"

Pull them up gently, tie them in a bunch...

Wash and scrub them carefully...

And eat some
with your lunch!

"Carrots are very good for you...
...don't you know!"

Now carrots can be orange,

though some are almost blue!

You can eat them in a salad or

put them in a stew!

"Carrots are
very good
for you...
...don't you know!"

Carrots can be eaten raw, can be boiled, roasted or baked,

...but Mr.Willow's favourite is to bake them in a cake!

"Carrots are very good for you...

...don't you know!"

Now carrots help you to see in the dark and make no mistake...

Carrots ARE very good for you...

...so let's bake them in a cake!

Who can you see in the picture opposite?

Yes, It's Grandad Willow and Mr. Willow when he was a baby... but you have to look very carefully to see them, don't you?

Now let's say the rhymes again... Can you join in?

Carrots are very good for you... don't you know!

Down in his garden, neatly in a row
That's where Mr. Willow's crunchy carrots grow
Carrots are very good for you... don't you know!

He sows the seeds and waters them well
Out comes the sun, and the seeds begin to swell.
Up pop the shoots; the leaves begin to grow.
Carrots are very good for you... don't you know!

Pull them up gently, tie them in a bunch
Wash and scrub them carefully, and eat some with your lunch!
Carrots are very good for you... don't you know!

Now carrots can be orange, though some are almost blue
You can eat them in a salad, or put them in a stew!
Carrots are very good for you... don't you know!

Carrots can be eaten raw, can be boiled, roasted or baked
But Mr. Willow's favourite is to eat them in a cake!
Carrots are very good for you... don't you know!

Now carrots can help you see in the dark
So make no mistake, carrots ARE good for you
...so let's bake them in a cake!

If you would like to hear this rhyme on YouTube please search for Carrots are very good for you don't you know! by Mr. Willow.

Let's make some really delicious carrot cakes with Mr. Willow.

Carrot Cakes

Ingredients

- 200g/7oz self-raising flour
- 100g/3oz grated carrots (cook in a covered bowl and microwave on full power for 1-2 mins. to soften)
- 150g/5oz brown sugar or 100g/3oz sugar and 50g/2oz maple syrup
- 2 tablespoons butter or sunflower margarine
- 2 free range eggs
- 50g/2oz raisins or sultanas

For the topping

- 100g/3oz soft cream cheese
- 30g/1oz icing sugar
- A little grated chocolate or cinnamon for the top (optional)

You will need:

Scales
Sieve
1 Large mixing bowl
1 small mixing bowl for the eggs
1 wooden spoon
1 tablespoon
1 fork or small whisk
1 muffin or bun tin
Paper cases (muffin or bun size)

Instructions

- **Preheat** the oven to 180°C/350°F/Gas Mark 4
- **Prepare** all the ingredients. Crack and beat the eggs.
- **Sift** the flour and cinnamon together.
- **Place** all the ingredients into a mixing bowl and stir until fully mixed.
- **Place** the mixture into cake or muffin cases and then into the oven.
- **Cook** for 20- 25 minutes until golden brown and "springy" to touch.
- **Place** on a cooling rack.

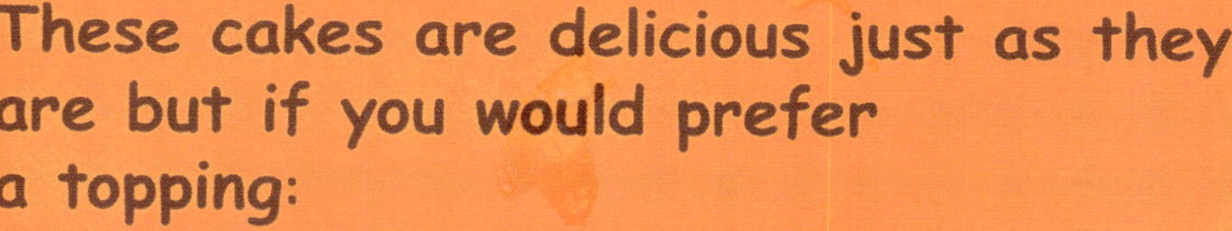

These cakes are delicious just as they are but if you would prefer a topping:

- **Beat** all the ingredients for the topping together using a bowl and a wooden spoon.
- **Spread** a little of the topping over each of the cooled cakes.
- **Sprinkle** lightly with grated chocolate or a "dust" of cinnamon.

Can you name any of the other fruits and vegetables that grow in Mr. Willow's garden?

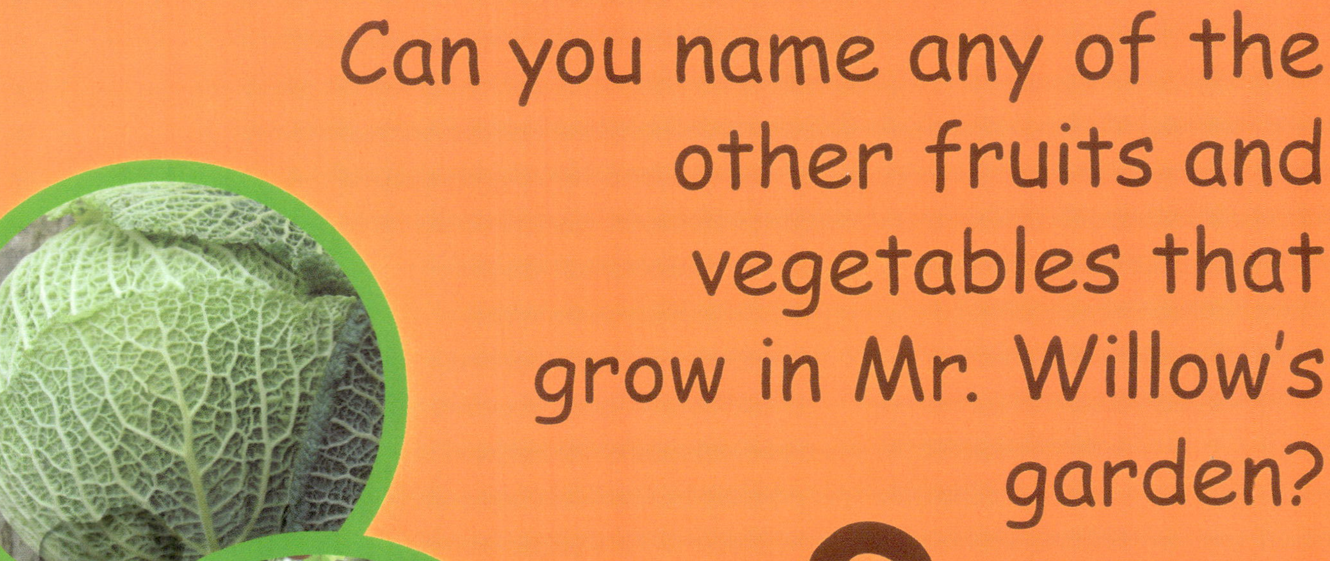

All of these grow **above** the ground (There are apples, blueberries, tomatoes, kolhrabi, courgettes, strawberries, grapes, plums and cabbage).

Kolhrabi

Blueberries

Apples

Strawberries

Courgette

Grapes

These cheeky rabbits live under Mr. Willow's shed!

They like to eat Mr. Willow's carrots because they are so tasty!

This is the tunnel that they have made under Mr. Willow's shed to pop in and out of their burrow.

Look at Pinky and Perky the spotty pigs.

Can you see what they are eating?

Yes... they are eating crunchy carrots for their dinner!

Can you see what Willy Wombat is eating?
Yes... a tasty carrot for his supper.

Photograph by Laura Salway

Murphy the black Labrador and Sooty the Labradoodle puppy love eating carrots too!

"But do you know WHY all these animals are eating carrots?"

Yes!... because carrots are very good for them... don't you know!

Can you count
some carrots
with Mr. Willow?

1
2
3
4
5

1 2 3 4 5 6 7 8 9 10

Mr. Willow's "under the ground" vegetable hunt.

All of these vegetable grow under the ground.

How many do you know?

Take this list with you when you next go shopping and see how many you can find.

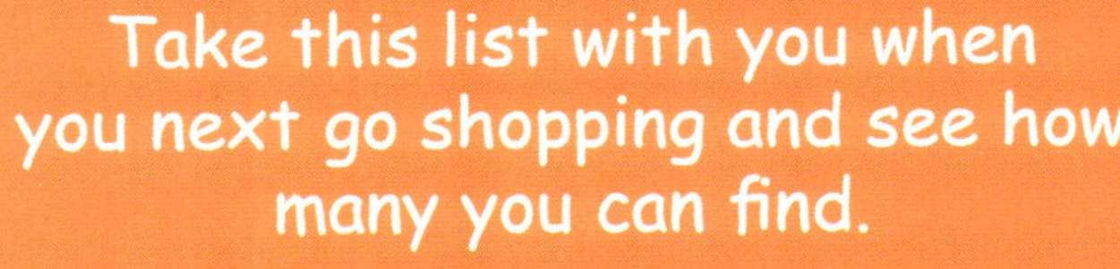

Which ones have you tasted?

Try some new flavours soon... they are all very tasty! You can even make your own special recipe for soup.

Vegetable	Tick if found	Tick if tasted
Carrots	☐	☐
Potatoes	☐	☐
Raddish	☐	☐
Parsnip	☐	☐
Yucca or Cassava	☐	☐
Turnips	☐	☐
Beetroot	☐	☐
Swede	☐	☐
Celeriac	☐	☐

Here are some more "carroty" ideas and activities for you to try

- Can you grow some carrots from seeds? Maybe you can even find some "rainbow" coloured carrots to grow!

- Can you find some more recipes and other ways to eat carrots? Carrot soup is very tasty!

- Can you make some carrot or vegetable people or animals? Have a look at some of the pictures.

- Carrots are called root vegetables. They grow under the soil. Can you find any other "root" vegetables at the shops or your farmer's market? Why not try Mr.Willow's "Under" the ground vegetable hunt on page 42 & 43.

- Can you use the ruler on the side of the page to measure some carrots?

- Can you see how long they are? Which is the longest carrot and which is the shortest?

watering
can

Other Mr. Willow Story and Activity Books:

- Mr. Willow's Herb Garden and Some Very Cheeky Seagulls!
- On the Beach
- All Kinds of Boats

Mr.Willow's Recipe Books

- Mr. Willow's ABC of Cooking WITH Children
- Mr. Willow's ABC of Cooking FOR Babies and Children
- Mr.Willow's Essential Recipes for Nursery Schools

For more "Foodie" educational resources for children please visit www.nurseryfood.com

About the author: Valerie Grady is Founding Director of Education and Child Development at Willow Cottage Nurseries, Oxford. She has 28 years experience in delivering excellence in Early Year's education and is an expert in her field of consultancy and mentoring in the reliable delivery of healthy food and fun food education to nursery children. Valerie holds a Food Science Honours Degree, a Post Graduate Certificate in Education and has been awarded the Government's cutting edge award to Early Years Professional Status (E.Y.P.S.)

Valerie has now published her proven and highly recommended way of delivering healthy home-made nursery food and fun food education for all children. Mr. Willow, "The Bear Chef " has been created as a children's food hero to make learning and understanding healthy food more fun for children. The Bear Chef's stories and poems will support you in the education of your child and have a simple and practical recipe for your child to make and enjoy afterwards...... with a little help from you of course!

CPSIA information can be obtained
at www.ICGtesting.com
Printed in the USA
LVIW012338101012
3088LVUK00002B